The Dog Show

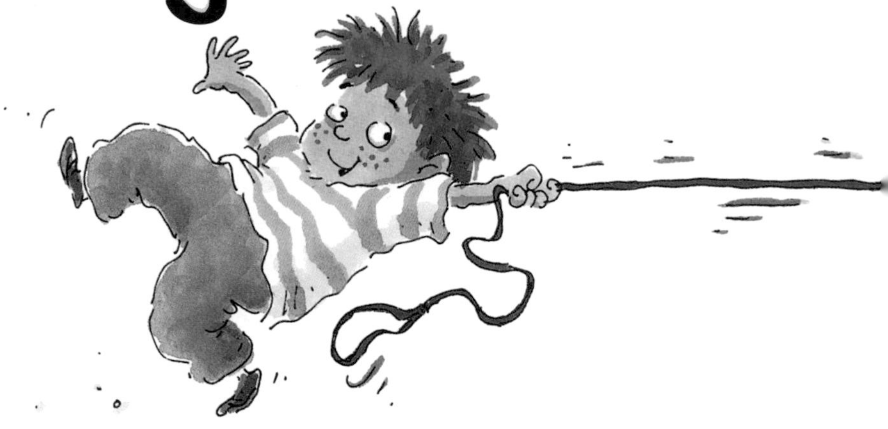

Barbara Mitchelhill
Illustrated by René Williams

RIGBY

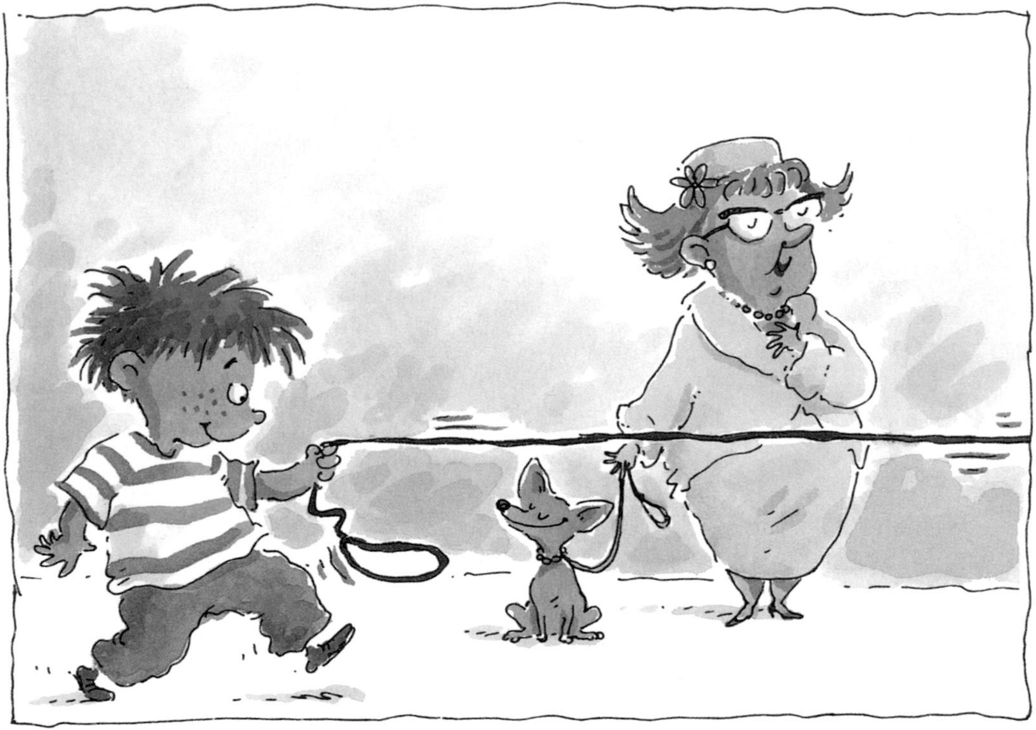

I like the little dog.

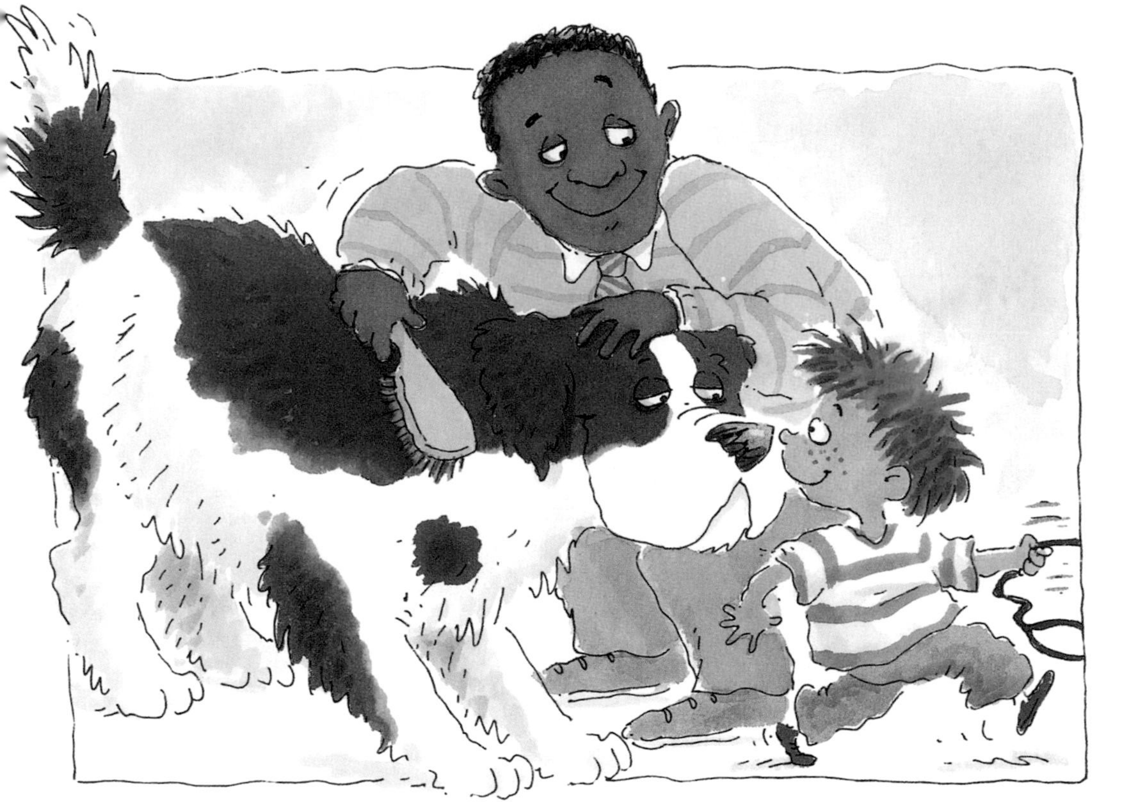

I like the big dog.

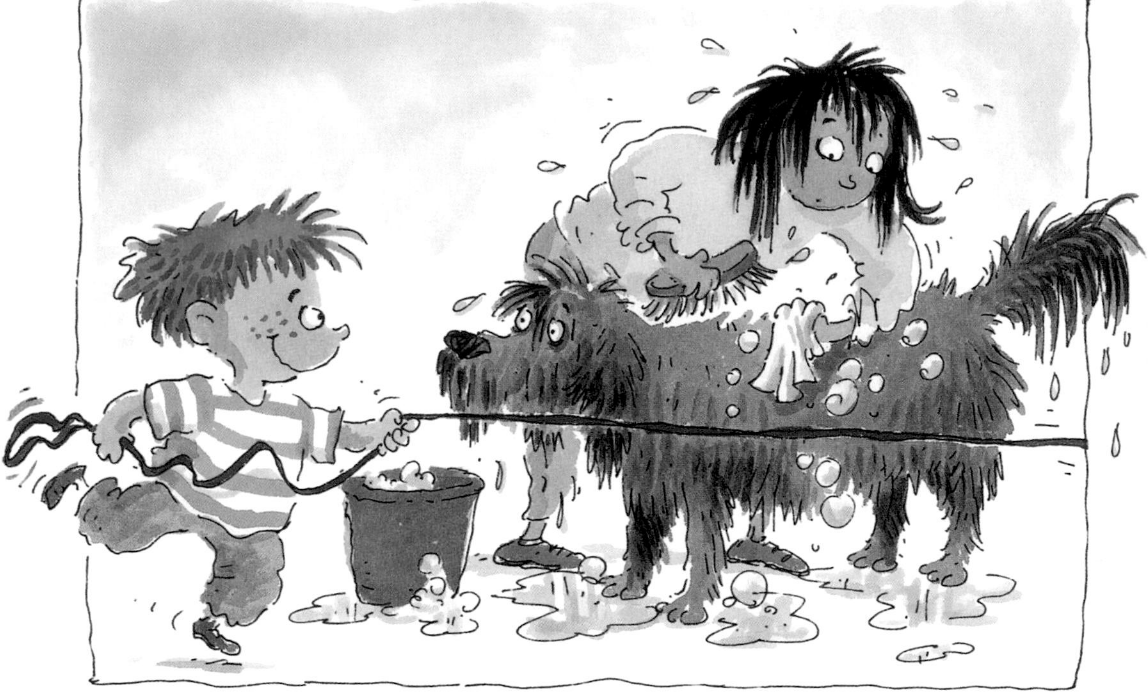

I like the wet dog.

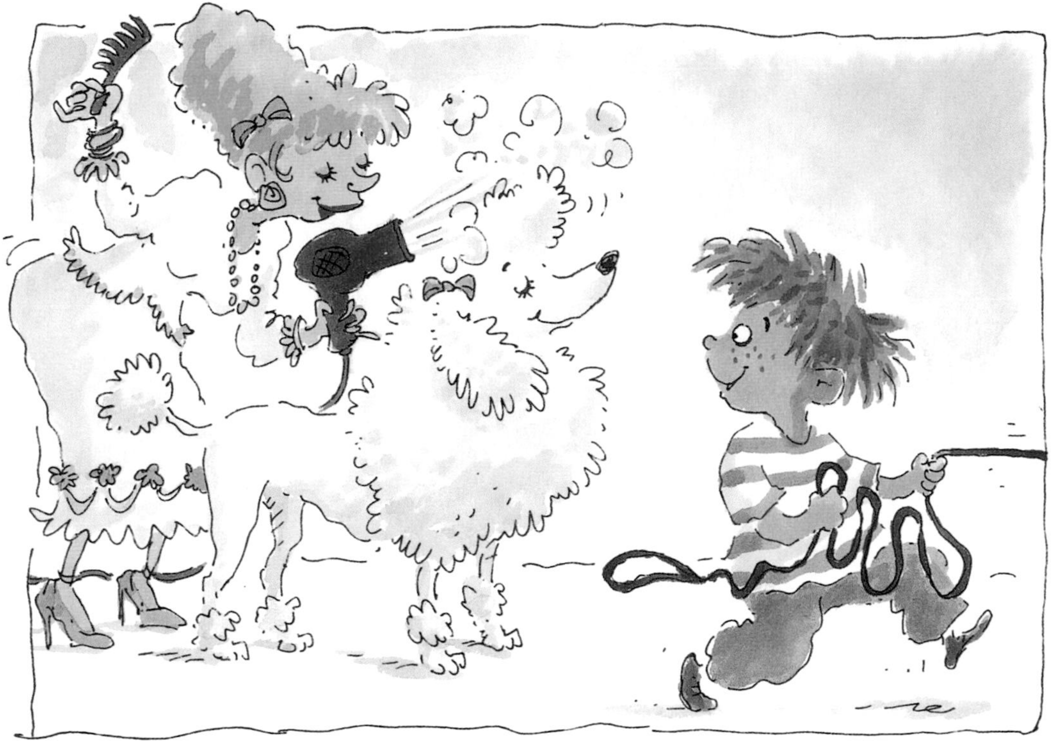

I like the dry dog.

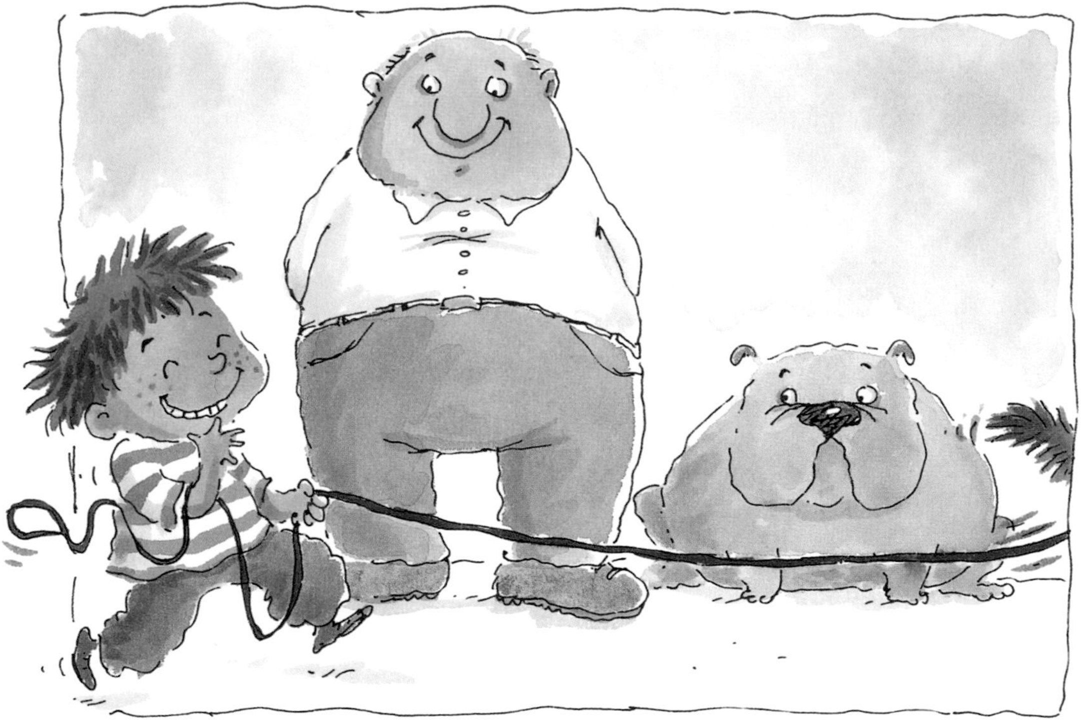

I like the fat dog.

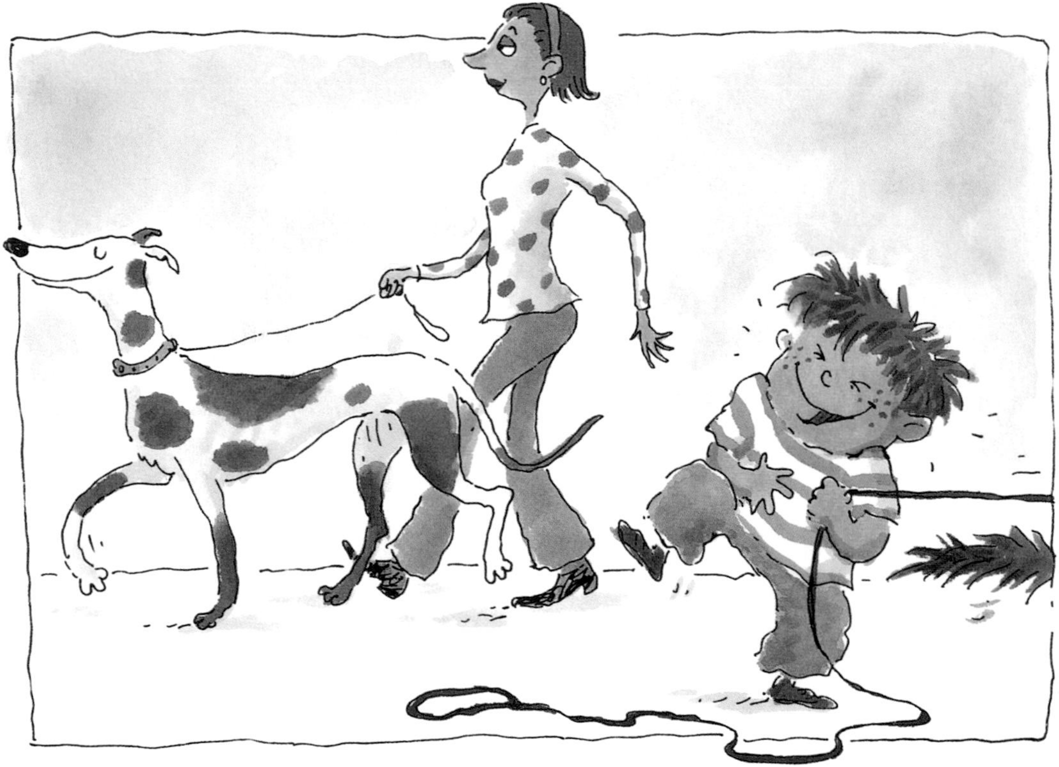

I like the thin dog . . .

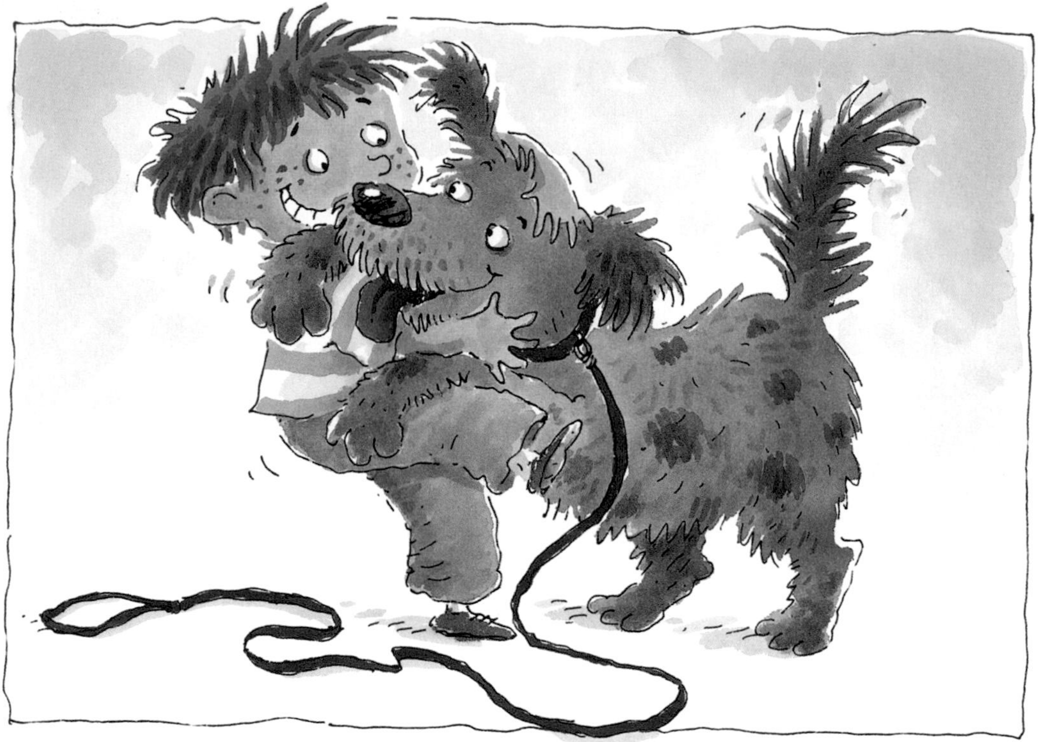

but I **love** my dog!